on the night of the
SHOOTING
STAR

illustrated by

AMY HEST . JENNI DESMOND

Bunny and Dog live on opposite sides
of the fence.

Bunny's house is blue.

A sign on the letterbox says

BUNNY HOUSE PRIVATE

Inside are a table for dining, a bed for sleeping, a lamp for reading and cocoa. Lots and lots of cocoa.

Dog's house is red. A sign on the door says

DOG HERE DO NOT DISTURB

Inside are a table for dining, a bed for
sleeping, a lamp for reading and biscuits.
Lots and lots of biscuits.

Every morning, first thing, Bunny looks
through the fence and the tall grass at Dog.

And every morning, first thing, Dog looks
through the fence and the tall grass at Bunny.

No one says hello. Or hi. Or nice to see you today.

Bunny hops

and nibbles
all through
the day.

She plants a carrot seed
here and there

CRUNCH
CRUNCH

and peeks at Dog.

When night comes, she sips cocoa in bed and reads.
Now and then she checks on the light in the window
of the little red house.

CARROTS
yum yum →

Dog skips and sniffs
all through the day.

He hides his ball

and digs it up

and peeks at Bunny.

No one says hello. Or hi. Or let's have a picnic today.

One sleepless night, Bunny goes out to the
garden to watch the stars above the little red house.
Dog's house. *Dog needs a friend,* she thinks.
Who could be Dog's friend?
The stars are dim but beautiful that night.

On the other side of the fence that very night, Dog
watches the moon above the little blue house. Bunny's house.
Bunny needs a friend, he thinks. *Who could be her friend?*
The moon is beautiful. And the stars.

All at once, the night sky brightens.

A shooting star!

ZZZZIP!

And then it is gone.

Bunny looks at Dog.

Dog looks at Bunny.

They had seen a shooting star.

But now it is gone.

Back in the little blue house, Bunny lies under
the table and thinks about Dog.
And their shooting star.

She thinks for a long time.

In the little red house, Dog sits on
the chair and thinks about Bunny.
And their shooting star.

He thinks for a long time.

On the night of the shooting star,
two doors open.

Bunny carries cocoa in cups, carefully,
to the fence, where Dog is waiting with
a basketful of biscuits.

"I could be your friend," says the one.
"Yes, please!" says the other.

They get to work digging a hole
under the fence.

In time it is just the right size
for the one to slip through

and just the right size for the other.

The cocoa is hot, the biscuits sublime.

They had seen a shooting star, and now it was gone.

But for the rest of their days and nights,
Bunny and Dog are exceptional friends.

For a couple of world-class readers,
Lily and Gabby, with love
A.H.

For Rachel, my lifelong friend who I admired
from afar when we started school aged four
J.D.

First published 2017 by Walker Books Ltd, 87 Vauxhall Walk, London SE11 5HJ

This edition published 2018

2 4 6 8 10 9 7 5 3 1

Text © 2017 Amy Hest
Illustrations © 2017 Jenni Desmond

The right of Amy Hest and Jenni Desmond to be identified as author and illustrator
respectively of this work has been asserted by them in accordance with the Copyright,
Designs and Patents Act 1988

This book has been typeset in Sabon

Printed in China

British Library Cataloguing in Publication Data: a catalogue record for this book is
available from the British Library

ISBN 978-1-4063-7937-2

www.walker.co.uk